Midnight & Mergers

MIDNIGHT RISING SERIES
BOOK FOUR

AMANDA KIMBERLEY

For my Family

About Midnight & Mergers

A Contract With A Clause Sealed With a Kiss...

Teagan was on her last nerve with men. The last one, especially since he kicked her out of her own apartment and fired her from her dream job. Now that she was nearing her mid-thirties, there was no way that she'd move back with her uncle. Once her 401K check came, she used it for the best condo she could afford in lower Manhattan. While in search of a new job, she found an unlikely perspective as an administrative assistant to one of New York's wealthiest moguls.

Being a glorified secretary was the last thing this marketing executive wanted. But rent would come after the holidays, so she didn't hesitate when Brooks handed her an employment contract. Once she reads the fine print of her contract, will she want to stay and cash in on the clause?

Brooks had little patience for friends and less for love as a vampire. His pet peeve was women throwing themselves at the thickness of his wallet.

When Teagan walked into his office, he cast caution aside and hired her because he was smitten. But the wealthiest man in New York couldn't crack under pressure. So would a Christmas Clause in her employment contract change everything?

Chapter One

"You've got to be kidding me! I'm the one whose name is on the lease. Why are you kicking me out? You should be the one leaving, Jeremy."

"Like you could afford this place? You don't have a job anymore."

Teagan's eyes widened, and she sucked in a breath.

"Are you saying you are going to fire me? That's really rich coming from you. I made your company the success it is!"

"I'm with Leslie now. You know that. And she's a

better marketing manager than you are. Plus, you haven't been the most professional at work lately."

"Why is she better? Is it because her boobs are bigger?" Teagan crossed her arms in an attempt to hide her B-cup from his view. It was silly on her part since he'd already sampled the goods for just over a year. She let out a clucking sound with her lips before continuing. "And you say that I am the one being unprofessional? Must I remind you how I found out you were cheating on me? You were fucking her on your desk in the middle of the day, for cripes' sakes!"

"And you should understand the common practice of knocking before you enter another person's office! You should also be aware that the practice of throwing things at your boss is assault and battery!"

"Oh, please! It was a stapler, and you ducked. I made my point. No harm, no foul."

"Look—this isn't working—you must get that. And if you leave quietly, I won't blackball you from the industry. Lord knows I've got every right to do so after you smeared, 'Leslie is the boss's slut.' all over the bathroom walls."

"You can't fire me just because you think I did that! Prove it!"

"I can fire you. And I don't need the proof. You are the only one bitter enough to want to write that. Plus, the assault alone is more than enough to fire you." He said to her as he handed her a weekender suitcase. "Take enough of your clothes for the next few days, and when you find a place, I'll have the rest of your things sent, including the furniture and the furball. I can't use any of the furniture since Leslie is allergic to cats. The fur is embedded in everything, so none of it will do. And obviously, you will need to make arrangements for the furball quickly."

Teagan closed her mouth, which had been agape for his entire speech.

"You can't be serious! This is ridiculous, Jeremy."

"It's not ridiculous. And I am serious. I promised Leslie you'd be out by tonight. You can't be here because of the restraining order I had her put on you after the stapler incident anyway."

"Yet another load of crap! You couldn't get that restraining order if you didn't pal around with a few cops and lawyers here in New York. One day there's going to be someone in your life that you can't fit in your back pocket. I hope I bear witness to such a monumental event."

Jeremy shrugged and pushed the weekender bag into Teagan's hands.

"It pays to have friends in high places."

"Don't you mean low? Because you've stooped to protozoan levels at this point."

"Teagan, I don't have time for your sulking or tantrums. Get your shit and get out of here, or I'll call the cops, and they can escort you out in a set of bracelets—your choice!"

"Fine! I'll go!"

Teagan entered the bedroom and found he had already packed her clothing in boxes. It wasn't that she had a lot of clothes, but seeing box after box lined up against the wall made her heart drop to her stomach. Bile seemed to have digested the poor thing because a hole started to form in the cavity where her heart once was beating. Her eyes welled, and she shut them immediately.

There is no way in hell that I'll let that ass see he has gotten the best of me!

She balled her fists and headed to the boxes. Jeremy had labeled each one of them in detail. She rolled her eyes and let out a sigh as she approached the nearest box.

Leave it to Jeremy to label all of my boxes thoroughly. At least I don't need to look in the boxes labeled evening wear. Probably won't need a ball gown for this Christmas season.

She peered in the box with business attire written over it and then rummaged through the box with undergarments labeled on it. Teagan picked out her best suit—she'd need it for interviews and grabbed her comfier bras and panties. At this point, she didn't have to bother with the sexier ones because she wasn't in the mood to even impress her Burmese cat, Morpheus. Not that he'd care—he was a cat, and the only thing that pleased him was running around the condo in the middle of the night singing the song of his people.

"Morpheus! Where are you, boy?"

She heard a mew from him before he stroked her legs.

"Come hell or high water, you, my dear, are

4

coming with me tonight! I don't care if we stay in a hotel for the next week—you are coming with me, boy!"

She gave him a good scratch behind the ear before she continued to shove more clothes in her weekender bag. Once she was done, she grabbed Morpheus's carrier from the linen closet, and he hopped in with a loud purr. A welcomed sound to Teagan because it signified that he was happy to leave with her.

Well, at least one male in this house still appreciates me!

She sucked in a breath and opened the door to head toward the condo's living room.

"You don't need to take Morpheus tonight. I can keep him until you find a permanent place of residence."

"That's quite alright. We both know he'd rather be with me than you."

"True. That cat isn't very fond of me."

"He tolerated you because he loves me—truth be told. Anyway, I'll email you my address once I find a place, and then I'll set up a UHaul."

"Sounds fine, but don't draw this out. I'm giving you only one week to find suitable arrangements."

"You cheated on me, you're firing me, kicking me out of my place—and yet—you've got the audacity to give me that kind of ultimatum? Your parents should've named you Richard because Dick would have been an appropriate nickname for you. Goodbye, Jeremy. Can't say it was a pleasure because clearly, this breakup is like you fucking me without the lube." She said as she placed the condo key in his hand. She slung her bag over her shoulder, turned on her heel, and walked out the door without saying another word to the asshole.

When Teagan got to the elevator, she let out a breath she didn't even realize she was holding in. She figured tears would soon follow the breath, but to her dismay, she was too pissed at him to cry. The ride down to the main floor was quiet. Even Morpheus seemed tired from the ordeal and was fast asleep when the doors opened to the main floor. Teagan let out another sigh and headed out onto the street. She hailed a cab and had the driver take her to the nearest hotel that allowed pets. Once she was settled, she dialed Em, her best friend she's had since middle school.

"GIRL! YOU KNOW YOU COULD CRASH AT MY place."

"Thanks, Em, but I didn't want to bother you. Plus, I've got Morpheus and know Derik is allergic."

"Okay, so where are you staying? Because I'm coming to visit you with the essential breakup meal of ice cream and wine."

"I'm at Club Quarters Hotel near the World Trade Center. Figured I might as well stay in the thick of the

Financial District so I could start pounding the pavement tomorrow. I booked the room for a week for a steal. Mark helped me out with the friend and family discount."

"Even at a discount, living in a hotel, Teagan, will get very pricey."

"I know, and if I really need to, I'll move back in with my uncle. But I'd rather avoid that at all costs. The last thing I need is for him to smother me, and plus, he creeps me out when he talks about the family secret."

"First, he means well, and second, your family secret isn't exactly easy to take in. I wouldn't believe you if I didn't see you shift into a kelpie horse myself."

"I know, but I'm not a kid anymore. It's time I stand on my own two feet—regardless of what my uncle keeps telling me about being a hybrid. Besides, this is a human problem and not a magical one."

"I hear you. Listen, give me 20 minutes to get there. I will stop at the packie and grab a nice bottle of cab."

"Okay, sounds good, but make it a big one."

"For you? I'll get a box!"

Teagan shut off her phone and let out a breath she'd been holding during their conversation. Emily was there for every breakup, every tear. But somehow, Teagan didn't have any tears or even fucks to give Jeremy. He was her worst mistake, and all she wanted to do was put him where he belonged—in her past.

It wasn't long before Em showed up at the hotel.

She met her in the lobby, and Em pulled her in for a hug.

"I couldn't find any suitable ice cream, so I settled on the big box of wine instead."

"That's fine with me. I would have wanted wine-flavored ice cream anyway." Teagan said with a chuckle. "I'm on the first floor—come on."

Teagan led her bestie into her room and grabbed the plastic tumblers off the bathroom counter. At the same time, Em fumbled with the perforation on the box. Once the spout was out, she poured a glass and handed it to Teagan.

"So what happened? The last time we talked, things were getting weird with Jeremy, but you didn't know he was cheating on you yet."

"These past couple of days have been a whirlwind. I mean, it was such a shock to see Jeremy fucking the new intern, Leslie, on his desk."

Emily took a sip of wine as her eyes widened.

"No way! You had walked in on them? What did you do?"

Teagan nodded and bit her lip before responding.

"The only thing I could. I flung a stapler at the ass."

"Shut up! Wait—why a stapler?"

"It was what I had in my hand. So I chucked it at him."

"Well, I hope it hit him. But honestly, chucking a stapler wouldn't be my first choice. I would have grabbed him by the balls and twisted." Emily said with a chuckle.

"Yeah. But hindsight is 20-20 because that rat bastard had Leslie slap a restraining order on me. They served me today at work. And just as soon as Jeremy's cop buddies did it, he had security escort me out of the building. Then when he came home, he kicked me out of the condo and fired me."

"What a dick!"

"Yeah, he sure is. I even told him his parents should have named him Richard because he truly passes as a Dick with a capital D."

"Oh, my God! I wish I were there to hear that coming from your mouth." Emily snorted between giggles.

Teagan smiled and then patted Emily on the shoulder.

"Thanks for coming tonight."

Emily tapped Teagan's hand on her shoulder.

"Of course! That's what friends do."

Chapter Two

Teagan's alarm on her phone went off as it always did every morning at 5 am. The blaring sound made her dart up from her sleeping position because she wasn't expecting it to come so early. She turned off the God-awful sound and groaned as she shuffled out of bed towards the bathroom. Morpheus gave her the side-eye as she shuffled by, signifying his disapproval of disturbing him at such an ungodly hour. She chuckled as she shuffled past him because he was always the one up at 3 am doing laps around the condo and singing the song of his people.

Not that any of the female cats could hear him 20 stories up. But he still enjoyed the prospect of wooing some fellow feline at the witching hour.

He hadn't had his man parts since he was 6 months of age, which is why the catcalls were hilarious. Just like his human counterparts—it didn't matter if nothing was virile down there. He still had the hots for the pussycats. Morpheus stroked against her legs as she padded out of the bathroom and into the central area of the bedroom. She was grateful this hotel had a coffeemaker inside the room. Because the one thing she hated the most about being in a fancy hotel room was getting dressed to grab a cup of coffee in the main lobby.

Once the cup finished brewing, she placed the sweet nectar onto the desk in the room and opened up her laptop to scour the hiring sites to look for a decent job that would pay rent. One particular job kept showing up in her search field, no matter what hiring site she was on. At first, she dismissed it because it was an administrative assistant position for a CEO. She didn't need another arrogant and rich asshole in her life, thank you very much. Then thoughts of Jeremy flooded her mind, and Teagan frowned.

Asshole.

"Crap! I don't want to be a glorified personal assistant, but this seems to be the only job looking for someone right away. At least the pay is decent."

She said this out loud to Morpheous before starting the application process. Once the main questions were answered, she was immediately asked to call for an initial phone interview. As she talked to the human resource woman, who sounded like she was in her mid-thirties, Teagan relaxed, and the interview flowed more like a chat.

"Can you come for a second interview this afternoon, Teagan?"

Teagan glanced at her computer to check the time. It was just past 10 in the morning, and she had plenty of time to get dressed and head to the interview.

"Uh, sure! What time?"

"Around 2 pm would be wonderful. Mr. Bradley will be back from his business lunch by then. You will do your second interview with him."

"Okay, that sounds perfect."

She hung up with Anne from the Human Resources department of the Bradley Corporation and let out a sigh.

"It's not my first choice. Frankly, it wouldn't be my twentieth. I'm so overqualified for this job, and it isn't even funny. But it'll at least give me some money for my rent. And right now, that's what I need the most. I just hope this guy isn't an asshole. But who am I kidding? Most CEOs are."

She then glanced at the condos for sale and found one she had completely fallen in love with on Wall Street. It was everything she had told Jeremy she wanted in a condo. Only he never wanted to indulge her. Not that they didn't have the money between them. It was more about him exuding his male dominance over her. She knew that her savings and 401K were substantial enough to even consider this dream of hers.

Before her interview, she called the realtor, who was happy to show her the place. She fell in love with the pool, the on-site gym, and the grey marble cascading countertops in the kitchen, and she almost didn't hesitate to put in an offer. Once the "virtual ink" was barely dry, she headed to Bradley Corp for her interview. She hoped to meet Anne because she got on swimmingly with her, but they escorted her to an office on the top floor and came face to face with the man she was supposed to have her final interview with.

"Great. Hope he isn't an asshole. He's too hot to be one, so one can only hope."

She mumbled that under her breath before smiling at him. His eyes kept wandering from hers to her lips for the first few minutes of the conversation. But what made her the most uncomfortable was that she sensed he was a vampire, which made her nervous. No other vampire accepted her, ever. In fact, she never met a vampire that even got along with normal shifters. But her? She was an abomination just by being born half kelpie and half witch.

Before her, kelpies were strictly born male. But the witch side in her made her the first female kelpie. The vampire before her had the power to shapeshift. She could sense that magic dripping from him, but the worst part was that he could probably shift into a wolf, and that was something her father and uncle told her to run from. This man before was something else, and the more she seemed to squirm in the seat and cross her legs, the more this vampire undressed her with his eyes. She had a cloak over her aura, so the hunger in the vampire's eyes wasn't about her being a kelpie.

Fuck! He's attracted to me. Just my damned luck!

The intenseness of his eyes, the smell of his earthy scent, and the quirk of his smile all said he was attracted to her. And it seemed her body was singing in perfect harmony with what he was trying to sell her. Every fiber of her core told her she shouldn't get involved with a vampire, not even on a professional level. But she couldn't shake the hold this vamp had on her. With each hooded stare he gave her, a sense of warmth washed over her. For the first time since her father died, she felt less like a freak of nature and more like a normal human being. That was a strange feeling for a magical creature to have.

Chapter Three

"Have you ever heard of Bradley Space? We recently sent a rocket up to the Space Station a couple of weeks ago."

Teagan blinked, shifted from her chair position, and crossed her legs for what seemed like the hundredth time in the past five minutes. The man made her nervous, especially now when he was talking about rocket ships. All she focused on was the appendage between his thighs. She bet anything that rocket would go off if she had her way with it.

Ugh! Down, girl!

And now? Never in a million years did she figure she would be quizzed on current events during a job interview!

"Honestly, I don't keep up with stuff like that."

"What about Ribrick?"

"I'm sorry?"

"Ribrick is one of the newer robot vacuums out on the market."

"Yeah, sorry. Don't know much about robot vacuums. Morpheus, my cat, would disapprove, so you wouldn't catch me buying something like that. With my luck, he'd purposefully use it as his litter box." She blinked again and then let out a nervous laugh.

Shit! I probably shouldn't have said that!

"OKAY. I'VE NEVER HAD ANYONE SAY THAT before about my tech products."

"I'm sorry, sir. I really don't get out much, and I'm not much of a TV person. Most of my spare time is spent working."

Brooks peered down at the woman's resume again. It was the only thing he could do not to laugh. She was acting somewhat ditzy, and he couldn't tell if she was lying about knowing who he was or not. Most women would jump at the chance to be his secretary, especially since many assume it would get them close to his bed. But this one, though sexy as hell, was playing hard to get, and that confused the living hell out of him.

"I see here that you are well-versed in marketing."

"Yes! It's a passion of mine."

"Then I don't understand. I used Smith and Connor marketing before. In fact, our last campaign with you was about six months back. You've got to be a little familiar with the products."

"You must have dealt with Jeremy. He was the one that did all the pitches, and I was always the one working behind the scenes and coming up with ad campaign ideas and slogans. I even wrote a couple of jingles for a dishwashing detergent. It's all right there." Teagan said as she pointed at the bullet points about halfway down the page of her resume.

A flowery scent tickled his nose as her arm gently brushed his.

Can she be? No! Impossible! I would have sensed if she was a shifter. And I'm sure she would have mentioned she was by now if she knew I was a vampire. But that scent! I've got to hire her to sort this out!

"That makes more sense to me now."

"How so?"

"When I'd ask him questions specifically geared towards the pitch he'd made, he was always very vague. I pushed him once to meet his team, but he came up with one excuse after another why I couldn't. I guess he didn't want to let on that you were more familiar with my products and the pitch than he was." Brooks said as he glanced over the resume once more before continuing, "Well, as far as I'm concerned, you are overqualified for this position. But I'm going to offer you the job, anyway. You will be required to accompany me to several holiday parties. They are mostly black-tie affairs. However, a few will be white ties. They will require ball gowns for these events."

Teagan's eyes widened as his lips dripped all of the foreign-sounding words, and finally, after she heard ball gowns, she had to interject.

"Um, I don't think I own anything fancy enough for even a black-tie affair at the moment. I'm in the process of moving, and I have packed everything in storage." She crossed her legs again, but this time it was for lying. She hoped her face didn't give away the thousands of thoughts now swimming in her head.

Is this guy for real? Does he want a personal secretary or a damned escort? I get there are company parties, but I shouldn't be expected to go to all these things with him. Who does he think he is?

"Oh, you needn't worry about providing your own gowns for this. I will see that my personal shopper handpicks some dresses on Fifth Ave for you. And they will all be charged to your corporate credit account. I will have Anne draw up your employment contract.

Then at the same time you are signing your agreement, we can get the necessary information we will need for the corporate credit card." He glanced at his calendar before continuing, "Are you available tomorrow at 10 am to go over and sign the paperwork? If not, I can have someone send over the paperwork to where you are staying."

He clearly couldn't help himself. The words just kept flowing from his mouth. All he seemed to want to do was get to know me on a personal level, and with each word he spouted, it sounded more like he wanted to dress me up and date me. There's no way I'm a Barbie doll! But... I need this job. Fuck!

"I can just stop by tomorrow. No need to have someone drop the paperwork off. Besides, I'm staying at Club Quarters until my, uh, condo on Wallstreet is ready."

She swallowed hard. She knew the ink wasn't even dry on the lease agreement and background check she had just signed earlier. But since it was in upper Manhattan, she figured it would be in her best interest to at least mention she could understand the level of VIP he was discussing with her.

"Oh, I've heard great things about that development. There are a few that are just going on the market this fall. The contract for hire is more of a formality, and it's got the usual nondisclosure agreements. Nothing you really need to worry about."

"I'm sure that stopping by around 10 will be fine. I

don't want anyone to go through the trouble of stopping by Club Quarters."

"That sounds fine. Tomorrow, then." He said as he picked up his phone in the office and began to dial a number.

Teagan took that cue and began to stand up and extend her hand.

"Thank you, Mr. Bradley, for this opportunity."

HE WAVED HER OFF AS HE GOT ON THE PHONE. It was all he could muster because he couldn't remember the last time a woman made his dick strain at the zipper of his trousers. Her hair was perfectly in place, she had gorgeous sienna skin, and her cheeks reddened a beautiful shade of rose every time he made eye contact with her. The woman crossed her legs as often as he locked his eyes on hers, probably because he knew his gaze lingered over her lips a little too often during the interview. The seemingly innocent gesture of shifting her weight in the seat gave him flashbacks of Sharon Stone. She was his childhood crush after watching *Basic Instinct* for the first time when he was 13. The movie had come out a couple of years before he'd turned 13. According to his parents, he wasn't allowed to watch anything with an "R" rating. But that didn't stop him from watching it with his buddies. Of course, the thought of this woman before him was making him want to jerk off, and that wasn't something he'd thought to do since the days of Sharon Stone.

His parents were doting up until the point he became a full-fledged teen. By that point, they thought it best to ship him off to boarding school—his pureblood parents and what pleased them never seemed to co-inside with his own thoughts about family. His mother said he was going away to school because it was more about his constant mood swings and how she couldn't handle them. His father? Well, he thought the boarding school would toughen Brooks up and build great character. Brooks didn't care to leave. He hated being shipped to boarding school because he missed all of his friends in the neighborhood. But being able to watch any movie with any alcoholic beverage of his choice was one of the few perks he had while growing up away from home. Sadly, his father and mother were both right. He was building character, and he was prone to mood swings. The boarding school just made those traits worse when he was younger. It wasn't until he was a senior in high school that he changed his tune —and not because his parents told him to. Nope. He did that on his own.

When the woman in front of him bit her lower lip a couple of times before answering him, he thought he was becoming completely unglued. Just the slight pucker of her lips made him want to get up from his desk and kiss her as hard and as passionately as she'd let him. The twinge in his belly as she smiled at him was almost foreign. Women and friends eluded him with each passing year and with each zero that he began adding to his paychecks as he divested his portfolio. In fact, the last time he ever had a meaningful relationship with anyone of the opposite sex was when he was a young teen in boarding school. Things were so much easier back then—even if he thought he got a raw deal with his loveless parents.

Women only liked him for his bank account, and at this point in his life, he didn't need an adult dependent. He was far too successful to have some gold digger take his company away from him. It took him an entire decade to build it from the ground up, so he wasn't about to piss it all away to marry some woman that would most likely divorce him the first chance she got. Sure, there were prenups, but Brooks didn't even want to bother having the paperwork drawn up for the shallow woman at the galas he'd been attending over the years. He would never date anything that resembled his own mother.

He had been so disheartened that this was the second year he decided to completely swear off women as his New Year's Resolution. And up until now, he'd been doing quite well with his celibacy—because no. Nope! He wasn't going to expend any energy on tapping a woman with zero substance. He'd almost thought that his man parts didn't work because he hadn't felt the slightest attraction to anyone for a couple of years.

But this woman? She seemed so different from the ditzy women he met at the parties. It was making him want to break his resolution and ask her out. Her intelligence as she spoke alone made his dick hard—a major feat for any woman to do with this vampire. Many of the women he now knew had been married into money. And they weren't pursuing any job other than coordinating an event for a charity they rarely knew little about. Damned *Housewives* shows made all of these women of today think the press would be impressed with the money they wanted to throw about for the actual parties. Forget about the charity! No—they just wanted their names spewed across social media. Many of them put on an event to get their husbands a tax break and cure their boredom in life. They all lacked the substance he seemed to find in the woman sitting before him, sweating as he grilled her. And if he was being honest, he enjoyed doing it because her flowery scent intensified as he fired off each question.

The sad part was he didn't require an administrative assistant until after the first of the year. Most businesses slowed in December because companies focused on sales rather than acquisitions. But he really wanted someone intelligent enough to accompany him during all of the damned holiday parties. Last year they made him out to be the next Billionaire Buddhist Monk. He didn't need a date or an escort this year, but he wanted one because he was tired of all of the women driveling at his feet. He didn't need arm candy. He just wanted a colleague to come with him to carry on a conversation and be visible enough for the vultures to leave him alone. And he knew if he could make the events part of the job where this assistant would help plan and attend them as a strictly business affair, he could still maintain his celibacy. The problem was solved as far as he was concerned, and this woman fit the bill, which is why he jumped at the chance of hiring her.

But now all he had to do was convince himself that there was still a no vacancy sign up around his dick.

Chapter Four

"Just what kind of clause is this?" Teagan said as she stormed into his office, nostrils flaring.

At this point, she didn't care if the Pope himself was in Brooks's office. He wasn't getting away with contracting her as his personal Barbie doll—no matter how gorgeous he was. Who did he think he was?

"Gentleman, please excuse me for one minute," Brooks said to the men in the room before addressing her. "Miss Teagan Thompson is my new administrative assistant who starts tomorrow. Let me just handle a bit of her paperwork quickly."

He led her to the door and closed it as soon as she walked through.

"What is it you need to have addressed?" His voice was in a matter-of-factly tone, his eyes fixed on hers.

"I thought this job would entail setting up your business schedule and writing up some spreadsheets. You didn't say that I'd have to plan these parties that you are telling me are mandatory to attend. And what's this 'fraternizing' bit? I mean—do you think I'd be the type of woman to fall in love with my boss just because I'm going to dinner parties with him? Sure, you're hot and dressing me up like a Barbie doll, but God, get over yourself." Her eyes widened, and she cupped her mouth. "I'm sorry. That came out wrong." She muffled out the words through her hand. He gave her a half-smile as his eyes flicked to her hand.

"That was an interesting choice of words." He chuckled before continuing. "Don't worry. I won't hold them against you. And as I explained to you yesterday, yes, I'd need you to accompany me to many gala affairs this holiday season. That will be part of your job this month. As far as fraternizing goes—that's a pretty standard clause in any company contract. Granted—the placement of the wording may have been off, and I can understand your concerns. But I can assure you that I have no ill intentions. Just your standard contract."

"Okay, but what is all of this other stuff? Why do you have to approve my wardrobe for these events?"

"Well, I'll be paying for the dresses. Therefore, I'll need to approve the garments to ensure they are suitable for the event."

"Okay, fair. But what about this? It says you may alter my work schedule to suit your needs. I thought this was an executive administrative position, not a personal assistant."

"That's in there because you will accompany me to set up some of the gala events. I may need you after hours for food tastings. It's hard to plan the menu we will serve without sampling it first. And I'd like to ensure the chosen venues have appropriate decor. For instance, I host an autism awareness event yearly, and I'd want to ensure that the venue uses splashes of blue in the decor for such an event. Look, Teagan, I assure you this contract is nothing out of the ordinary. But if it makes you feel better, have your lawyer look this over, and you and I can discuss the contract over an early dinner today. I'll have my car pick you up around 4. Consider this a welcome aboard dinner. Oh, and wear a cocktail dress. I'll be taking you to my favorite place—L'appart."

His eyes seemed to twinkle. Or was there a glow of silver around the pupil? She tried to get a better look, but her sightline to his gaze became blocked as he casually peered at his watch. He looked up again, and his eyes pierced hers. They were now both a light blue. The silver was a distant memory, but they were still mesmerizing and playful with her as they flicked from her gaze towards her lips. Her legs buckled at the mischievous glint in them. "Teagan, I must get back to my meeting. I'll risk a double booking if I run over my time with Mr. Jameson. Please bump my 1 pm to 1:30, and I'll meet you at the restaurant. The reservation is under Brooks Bradley. I'll be there by 4:15-4:30 at the latest."

Teagan opened her mouth, but before anything came out, he was already back in his office, apologizing to the business executives there. She blinked a couple of times before Anne came up to her.

"Come with me, and I will show you to your desk so you can shift his appointments around." Her smile was bright and beaming as she gestured for Teagan to follow her.

"Is he always like that?" Teagan tried to bite her lip to stifle all the verbal diarrhea that was about to slip through them if she wasn't careful. But clearly, it was already too late.

Usually, she could keep her feelings of annoyance to herself, but this man was getting the best of her—and not in a good way.

Standard clause, my ass! How can he think arrogance will get him everywhere in life?

Anne formed a half-smile on her lips before answering.

"I like you, Teagan, so I'm only going to warn you about our Mr. Perpetual Bachelor Boss. Keep things strictly professional with him, or you'll risk getting hurt. I'm not telling you what to do with your love life —please don't misunderstand. It's just? I've known him for years, and he's not the type to settle for anything. That, unfortunately, includes women as well."

Teagan narrowed her eyes.

"So, I was right to question all that nonsense with the *Christmas Clause* in my contract? Because seriously? The only merging that guy will do in my presence will involve companies he's planning on purchasing." She didn't want to stress the emphasis on the contract, but at this point, she felt she had no choice.

Anne shrugged her shoulders.

"That part is more of a bit of company policy than anything else. But hey, just be careful. Brooks's type is very gorgeous and flirtatious. And that usually spells a disaster for most of the young women in his life."

"So, what makes you stay?"

Teagan searched Anne's eyes for an answer. They were a brilliant green. The corners of her eyes were dotted with dark circles that almost seemed painted over her fawn complexion. A hint of crow's feet was faintly forming around them, signifying the wisdom behind her advice.

"He reminds me of my boys when they were his age. They are all in their late thirties, successful, married, and have blessed me with enough grandchildren to keep me busy for the next decade. I worry about Brooks, though, more so than I ever did with my children. He's got a great heart but holds it close to his chest, which can make him—" She swallowed before continuing. "cold—would be the best word for it. Teagan he's not exactly the easiest boss to deal with at times. Once you get past his façade, he's seriously misunderstood, and he's got a great heart and would do anything for his employees. I've been lucky enough to witness that firsthand." She smiled again and shifted her eyes towards the door.

Teagan let out a breath she didn't realize she was holding in.

"So what you're saying is—I'm in for a hell of a bumpy ride when it comes to his cold, dead heart?"

Anne smiled again as they entered the room. The desk, a rich mahogany, was facing the hallway, but the office's back wall was a floor-to-ceiling window with the backdrop of the New York City skyline. The walls were a deep rich hunter-green. Each wall opposite the large desk in the middle of the room flanked bookcases that were a deep mahogany brown that matched the desk.

The colors reminded Teagan of a cigar-smoking room. She figured Mr. Brooks Bradley had a say in the decor. But despite the dark tones of the rooms, it was a gorgeous upscale office that anyone would die for. The decor screamed, making it big. The only thing missing was that it wasn't the corner office, but it was damned close because the corner office was Brooks's. And oddly, only her and Brooks's office were on this side of the floor. That excited and terrified Teagan simultaneously because she'd have privacy from other staff members so she could focus on her work. But that also meant Brooks had the easiest access to her and could bug her whenever he wanted. The thought of him micromanaging her made her skin crawl. Her office and Jeremy's had the same setup when she worked with him. Back then, she didn't mind because they were happy. But Brooks wasn't Jeremy, and she was hoping to avoid the claustrophobic feelings with this new job.

"Honestly, Teagan, he's really not a bad guy. And for fear of having to tuck tail and run from this conversation—let's just say I'm here to make sure he keeps his humanity intact when it comes to his nasty side." She smiled again, only this time it seemed warmer. She then patted Teagan's shoulder before pulling a large calendar from the desk's middle drawer. Anne's touch was just as friendly as her smile, allowing Teagan to feel more relaxed about her decision.

She knew her next job after Jeremy would not be easy, and she also knew she would not find something she'd want to do for the rest of her life. But Anne seemed to comfort her trepidations about this weird *Christmas Clause* arrangement enough that Teagan was willing to take this job for at least through the holidays. She could always find something better come January if she had to. If she could survive a cheater that drove her out of her home and fired her from her dream job, she could survive a boss with a calculating side to him.

33

Teagan put down her purse to fish out a pen. She then signed the contract and returned it to Anne.

Anne's eyes widened slightly as Teagan handed over the contract.

"Are you sure you want to sign this now? Mr. Bradley explained that he'd go over your terms during dinner."

"I'm confident we can make some addendums. That's how these things work—right? I mean, that's what I'm used to, anyway."

Anne's eyes narrowed slightly before answering.

"Are you sure?"

"I am. Besides, I really need this job. It's so tough finding one so close to the holidays, and I'm sure I can handle Mr. Grumpypants. After all, my last boss was Mr. Lyingcheat, so anything else is a step up in the perfect employment ideals—if you ask me."

Anne took the contract from Teagan and cradled it in her arms.

"Okay. I'll leave you with your phone calls. You'll also have to phone the restaurant and double-check the reservation for this evening. I don't believe the entire place is booked yet, but make that your first call, just in case. Most of Mr. Bradley's clients know his constant shifts in meeting schedules. He gets busy a lot. Oh! And I probably don't need to tell you this because you are familiar with the corporate world, but you may make this office your own. If you aren't happy with the paint color, just say the word, and I will get our contractors in here. The colors are dark and suited to the design styles of the prior executive assistant. You appear more like someone into a light and airy motif." Anne said with a wink.

"Yeah, I'm not really into the cigar-smoking decor." Teagan chuckled before continuing. "Thanks for everything, Anne. You've been so kind to me, and I hope we can become good friends here."

"I hope so, too," Anne met her gaze with a bright smile and then turned on her heel to walk out of the office.

TEAGAN SAT DOWN AT HER NEW DESK. THE chair, though gaudy for her taste because the front feet of the apparent accent chair had carved claw feet. But they weren't typical. The feet themselves seemed ornately unique. They didn't appear to be the normal lion ones she was so used to seeing in her father's study growing up. When Teagan was young, she asked her father why he seemed to be so obsessed with lion-clawed furniture. Even the guest on-suite that he retreated to once her mother, the love of his life, had died, had a claw-footed tub.

Not all of the decor in the room was adorned with clawed feet as an accent, and sometimes there were lion statues and vases with hand-painted lions on them. Much of Teagan's new office decor reminded her of her father, who passed two short years ago.

He was a wealthy man in his own right and had left Teagan a substantial amount of money that Teagan was able to invest. Her nest egg was more significant than most others at her age. Still, a good amount of the money was tied up in escrow. And she didn't want to piss away her father's legacy. She decided to enlist the help of her father's lawyer to keep as much of the family legacy in a trust fund. This way, she could ignore the investment until it matured in her retirement years.

"You are being silly, you know!"

"Really, father? Are we going to go there again? Why are you so cryptic about our family's heritage?"

Her father walked towards her in his study and cupped her cheeks.

"Teagan, as I've told you, you are an extraordinary girl. And as I promised your mother, I will look out for you until my dying breath. I hope you find someone else willing to protect you by then."

"Father! You need to stop being so mellow-dramatic about the 20th century. I don't need a man to be my knight! I'm more than capable of taking care of myself."

He stroked her right cheek before continuing.

"No one ever said you weren't capable of taking care of yourself. But should trouble arise in your life, I want you with someone that can help protect you from the people in life that don't understand just how special you are."

Teagan chuckled at her father's words.

"Father, really? Again with all this cryptic talk? Don't you think you should let me in on the family secret? I mean—I get we were cut off from your side. But you never told me what the feud was about." She said as she palmed her father's forearms.

"Princess, I told you—that feud is between me and my side. You have no need to be in it. You are an innocent when it comes to all of this."

"And there you go again, calling me an innocent! Father, you do realize that everything about my favorite TV show Charmed is make-believe—right?"

"I'm sorry, princess. I know I talk differently than what they do here in the States. But I'm Gaelic. What do you expect?"

Teagan squeezed her father's forearms again before pushing away from him.

"I don't understand anything about my Scottish heritage. You've been so reluctant to tell me anything. Mom was always so good about telling me about my Italian and Spanish roots. But you've been so tight-lipped."

"Princess, do you remember everything your mother told you?"

"Well, some of it is still a blur. I mean—she died

when I was seven. But I remember her using the word Strega a lot."

Her father cupped her cheek again and then stroked her hair.

"Yes, she did. And when I find where she and your grandmother kept their journals—I promise—you will have them. Hopefully, that puts some of the pieces together for you."

"You are still being the perpetual crypt-keeper, aren't you? What's a Strega?"

"Princess, you will come to learn what that means, along with everything else about my side of the family, soon enough."

"Right. Are we going to bring up the fact that I'm not old enough to know again? I mean—come on? At almost 25 years old, I am no longer a kid. I think it's time for you to fess up."

"Fine, Teagan. I will tell you. The TV Shows you love to binge-watch so much are based more on fact than fiction. You are a Strega Witch on your mother's side and a kelpie shifter from my side. That makes you a hybrid witch and a mighty powerful one because you are the first of your kind. Should anyone discover your secret, you will be forever on the run. Because both pureblooded werewolves and vampires believe hybrids are an abomination. Your mother and I wanted to protect you."

"Is that why we always moved when I was a kid?"

"Yes, Teagan. That is why."

Teagan shook her head while muttering to herself.

"You never got the chance to tell me why possessing a kelpie witch's power was so dangerous, father." She let out a sigh before continuing. "And you never told me how to figure out who I should be running from."

A knock came on her door, breaking her train of thought.

"I see you are becoming acquainted with your new office. Anne told me you are double-checking our dinner reservations and moving my schedule around. How is that going? Did you get a hold of Stevenson, Taylor, and Barnes?"

Teagan sucked in a breath. She hadn't called for the dinner reservation yet, and her boss was already assuming she was done with all of her tasks. He couldn't be done with his meeting so fast because she'd only been thinking of her father for a few short minutes.

Right?

"I'll get right on that, sir! I, uh, am looking for their numbers now."

Brooks frowned slightly.

"What have you been doing for the past half-hour,

then? Please tell me you've at least checked on the reservation for dinner." He said, as his nostrils began to flare.

Fuck! It hasn't even been a full day, and I'm already pissing him off!

Teagan bit her bottom lip.

"I, uh. Well, you see—"

Brooks's glare seemed to shift towards her lips as she bit down on them.

"It's okay." He said as he took in a breath and closed the distance between the two of them. "I shouldn't expect you to know where all the phone numbers are or anything. In all honestly, it isn't even your first day yet. I see the calendar out in front of you and just now realized I didn't have their phone numbers marked in it." He continued as he patted the blotter calendar on the desk. His fingertips grazed hers, and she felt heat surge through her entire body.

Damned kelpie senses! Stop tingling! He's not even my official boss yet!

"Don't worry about calling them. I'm already done with my first meeting, anyway. I have a few minutes to get everything set for L'Arppart. How about you head home and get ready for dinner? I will see you at 4." He turned on his heel and headed back to his office as if he were running a marathon and winning was all that mattered to him.

Chapter Five

Before he shut his door, she saw him pick up the phone and dial a few numbers. The muscles in his shoulders seemed to tense more and more the longer he was talking on the phone. He then slammed the door. Shouting blasted through it, but the tone was muffled enough that Teagan couldn't make out what he was saying. Teagan sucked in a breath and balled her fists.

What the fuck did I get myself into with this new boss? I can't have a weird crush on my boss—especially since he's a vampire! And with my luck, he's the enemy my father warned me about.

Teagan let out a shaky breath as some of the curse words her boss was yelling were finally audible.

Shit, he's pissed. And I get why—I fucked up, and it isn't even my first day. And why the fuck am I losing time again? Fuck! I hope no one saw me shift! This only happens when it's a full moon or my fated mate has appeared to me. Wait... Could he? No! Teagan. Stop it. That's not possible!

She raked her fingers through her pin-straight blonde hair and let out a shaky breath. Another knock at the door interrupted her thoughts, and her eyes darted to the door as she felt her face draining of color and feared that it was Brooks again.

"I'm sorry. I didn't mean to disturb you. Are you okay?" Anne asked as she rushed into the office and closed the door behind her. "What did he say to you?"

Teagan locked her eyes on Anne. She drew in a breath to calm herself before answering any of Anne's questions. There was no way in hell she would let Brooks get to her. She'd had enough of controlling and manipulative men—not that Brooks was like her nightmare ex. But? The man was throwing a colossal vampire tantrum.

She would not let her boss get the best of her— magically speaking or mundanely speaking. And none of that mattered compared to the time lapses. She couldn't have this happen to her again, especially since her father was the only one that could stop them from happening before. Now that he was gone, she hadn't the slightest clue what she would do. Her only option was to ask Uncle Jon, but since her father swore her to secrecy after the first bout of time lapses, she doubted her Uncle Jon would know anything. She surely didn't want to come across to Uncle Jon as being crazy because a trip to a rubber room wouldn't help her condition. That nickname was for the room Teagan had sometimes seen her father in during childhood. Uncle Jon used to say they padded it so her father could play racquetball. Still, as she grew older, she understood that room represented a safe place to give in to your animalistic side. The problem was that the room didn't work for Teagan. She was part witch, which meant she could astral project herself outside the room, making things worse for the people around her.

"It's nothing, Anne. He just got a little angry with me because I hadn't made any of the calls yet."

"But I left you half an hour ago."

"Yeah—I'm now painfully aware of that." Teagan's voice trailed, and she bit her lip. She wasn't about to tell Anne the truth. Not when the truth could get Anne hurt—or worse—give Teagan a one-way trip to looney-bin central. "I, uh, guess I got lost in thought while staring out the window. It's a gorgeous view." Teagan gave her a half-smile, hoping the lame excuse she just gave Anne would suffice.

Anne raised a brow.

"Yeah. I guess you aren't used to a cushy office, then?"

"Oh, yeah. My last job only had an office on the ground floor. Wasn't all that spectacular."

"That's unfortunate," Anne said with a half-smile. "Listen, the reservations are taken care of, so why don't you head home and get ready for dinner? Brooks has me bring the car to your place to pick you up."

"Uh, sure. That sounds great. Oh, please tell Brooks I'm sorry for screwing up on my not-quite first day."

She had just finished her apology to Anne when Brooks stormed out of his office.

"No need to apologize. I told you it's my fault— not yours."

His jaw seemed to tighten with each word until his steely gaze locked onto her. She bit her lip, and his eyes instantly softened as they flicked toward her lips.

"Still, I probably should have asked you for the numbers. And for that, I apologize." She gave him a half-smile and noticed his fists were balled up.

"Teagan, why don't you head out? I've taken the liberty of sending your dress to the hotel you are staying at, and you can pick it up at the desk. You're staying at Club Quarters—correct?"

"Yes, that's right, Anne."

Brooks sucked in a breath and pinched the bridge of his nose before responding.

"That sounds like a great idea. I'll see you at 4, Ms. Thompson."

TEAGAN SMILED AT BROOKS AND THEN GOT into the elevator. Once the doors shut, Brooks turned to Anne.

"Do you see what I mean about her scent? It's driving me insane! She has to be a shifter!"

"Yes, Brooks, I understand. The thing is, though, her aura doesn't exude the qualities of a shifter. I think she's more than less likely a human. A bit of a strange one because of the scent, though. I can't put my finger on why this is happening, but as far as I can tell, she's just human. I think. Truth is—I really don't know. My research this afternoon hasn't panned out. I'll dig deeper into her parents and see if I can find the link between her and shifters."

"But you get it—right? That essence is unmistakable! She's got to a shifter. There's no other explanation for this!" Brooks balled his fists again.

"Listen to me," Anne said as she palmed Brooks's shoulder before continuing, "you've got to get yourself under control! The last thing we need you to do is to vamp out in public. No one can know you are a vampire. I made that promise to your mother, and I intend to keep it!"

"Yes, Anne, I remember. We can't risk exposure. The humans don't know of our existence, and since I'm newer at this—I get why my mother entrusted you to help me once she was gone. But you admit that the damned Twilight glitter made it impossible for any actual human to believe in our existence." He grunted under his breath before continuing. "Listen, I've gotten Jameson on board, and I'll get Stevenson, Taylor, and Barnes on board as well. This girl, Teagan, is under the protection of my coven until we can figure out why she exudes the essence of a shifter. This isn't normal, Anne. She's in danger if the werewolves find her. And let's face it—she's in danger from any other vampiric clan, too. I want to get to the bottom of what is different about her before they do. Because I'd hate to think what they'd do to her to gain her powers."

"I understand. Tyler has been ruthless in the magical community since Keme approved of him watching over the New York territory. If a witch so much as talks with a shifter, there is hell to pay. That damned Common Trifecta Law will be the death of us all. But again, keep your cool! We don't want to scare Teagan off or make Tyler suspicious. He'll not only come after Teagan but me as well."

"Don't you think I know that, Anne? It's just—I haven't felt this way about a woman since, well, since?" He bit his lip before saying the one name he vowed never to speak of again. "Since Sarah." He let out a breath he didn't realize he was holding in.

Anne furrowed her brows.

"Are you trying to tell me that this girl, Teagan, might be your mate?"

"That's exactly what I'm saying."

Chapter Six

Teagan got to the bottom floor and hailed a cab. As she shut the door, all her pent-up emotions rushed through her again.

"Where to?"

"Club Quarters, World Trade Center, please."

"Sure thing!"

As the taxi pulled out into the street, Teagan bit her lip and stared out the car window. The streets of New York became a blur, as did much of what happened during her memory lapse.

How could I have lost that much time? I know I was

thinking about my father, but I couldn't have thought about him for that long! 30 minutes is far too long, so I must have shifted! It's the only explanation that makes sense. What am I going to do? My father was the only one that could keep my kelpie horse at bay!

Her thoughts suddenly turned to Brooks. Sure, she felt something for him. Her damned libido had been in overdrive since the minute she met him. But was he really going to be the answer she needed for her shifter side? He was a vampire—and most likely a pureblood. Father told her to hide from vampires like him. It was why she made sure her protection spell, the one that blocked purebloods from reading her, was in full force when she was in Brooks's presence. She just hoped her mojo was strong enough to keep Brooks and the rest of his employees in the dark.

And what's up with liking that guy, and why was I so stupid to call him hot? He's my damned boss now, for fuck's sake!

She buried her head in her hands.

God, how could I have been so stupid? It wasn't even my first day, and I was already calling my boss a hottie. WTF?

Thoughts of Jeremy flooded her mind, and all the betrayal came rushing back.

I can't do this. I will not make the same mistake twice. No more dating the boss, even if this one is a vampire that is most likely my mate!

The taxi came to an abrupt halt, jarring Teagan from her thoughts. Teagan paid for the cab and headed to the front desk, where a garment bag was waiting for her, along with a large bag containing a box that she assumed included a pair of shoes. She peered into the bag and found some unmentionables, to her surprise. She grabbed everything and headed to her room, where Morpheus greeted her with his usual mew. Annoyed that he was being disturbed from his nap, he began his other favorite pastime, the obsessive licking of his fur.

She walked straight towards the bed and carefully laid out the garment and shopping bag she retrieved from the front desk.

"Alright. Let's see if Mr. Brooks Bradley has any taste in women's clothing." She said to Morpheus as she unzipped the bag, pulled out the dress, and gasped.

She knew the dress designer without even having to gaze at the tags. It was an Oscar de la Renta made of black guipure lace and had a soft silk lining. The dress was elegantly stunning, with some carefully hand-sewn beaded sequins, making the monetary value of the clothing that much more expensive.

The thing was, she didn't have to guess the price of the gown. Teagan knew the dress was over three thousand dollars. One of her favorite past times was looking at the Saks Fifth Ave website and dreaming about all the gorgeous dresses she'd never be able to afford. This one happened to be one she'd been obsessing over for the past three months. She pulled the dress to her body and turned to the full-length mirror. The dress clung to her curves in all the right places and was the correct size, which should shock her. But the man had a hooded gaze over her during their entire interview, so she didn't doubt for a second that he didn't know every visible scar she had at this point.

"God, if this is the dress—what do the shoes look like?"

She opened the shopping bag and pulled out the shoebox that contained a pair of Manolo Blahnik black satin mules with crystal embellishments. And again, not so surprisingly, they were also the correct size. Vampires and their parlor mind-reading tricks, no doubt. But still? The man bore into her long enough that he probably saw her very soul. Just that thought alone left her feeling completely naked. The shoes themselves were over a grand, thanks to her obsessiveness with shoe searches on Saks. She had her eye on those very shoes, too. And all thanks to a suggestion to complete the look with the dress.

"Good Lord!"

She placed the shoes back on the bed and peered into the shopping bag again. She pulled out a Kiki de Montparnasse bralette with a matching thong. Those alone would add up to a grand in total. This man clearly didn't care how much he spent. And now she was wondering if her obsession with Saks was his, too. Or? Did he read her mind like an open book? Because clearly, this was borderline crazy that he already knew her this well. There was also a pair of pantyhose and a black clutch—two things she vowed not to search on Saks for. The main reason was the fear of realizing exactly how much he had spent on her before she had become an official employee. Teagan didn't want to know the actual price tag, especially once she found more in the bag.

Is this guy completely certifiable?

A large jewelry box appeared at the bottom of the shopping bag. Teagan opened the black velvet box, and it contained a diamond choker with some matching stud earrings. The necklace had too many diamonds on it to count. And the thing sparkled in the dim light so brightly that she could only assume she'd light up a room. The jewelry was far more expensive than the dress and the shoes combined.

"Oh, my God. I will have to get insured before I put this thing on!"

She dropped the box onto the bed and the dress and headed into the bathroom, turning on the shower.

"I'm going to have to chat with Mr. Braggy Brooks Bradley. He can't buy me stuff like this! This isn't a real-life Pretty Woman thing, and he's certainly no Richard Gere! What the fuck have I gotten myself into?" She yelled this to herself in her full-length bathroom mirror before hopping in the shower. The water from the showerhead beaded on her cheeks as she shut her eyes. "And how could he know my sizes? The dress is small, which wasn't too much of a stretch. I have a thin frame—but how'd he get the shoe size, right? It's like he really was undressing me with his eyes yesterday and today." Teagan shook her head to shake off the obsessing she was doing because if she weren't careful, she'd go back to thinking he read her mind. There was no way in hell she wanted to go there—not now—not ever. Because fuck no, that's just creepy! "Perhaps he had the maid rummage through my closet? But that's also a tad creepy!" She sighed, turned off the shower, and dried off.

After she got dressed, she was thankful that the hotel had a blow dryer that didn't frizz up her pin-straight hair. She then put on some BB cream, mascara, and burgundy-red lipstick and headed out the door. When she walked out of the hotel's front entrance, there was a man dressed in a uniform holding a sign with the name Teagan Thompson written on it.

"Hi, I'm Teagan Thompson."

"I'm here to take you to L'Appart, Ms. Thompson," He said as he led her to a stretched limo parked on the street. He opened the door for her, and she slid in.

Once the door was shut, Teagan mumbled under her breath, "So much for having the car come and pick me up. Who the fuck calls a limo a car? I guess Mr. Bradley does."

The driver's side opened, and the man got in and started to close the partition.

"Oh, you don't have to do that! I don't need any privacy. A stiff drink before my business dinner with Mr. Bradley, maybe. But I don't need any privacy."

The man smiled through the rear-view mirror.

"There's a bar in the corner over there. Mr. Bradley fills it with scotch, mostly."

"That's perfect, thank you, Mister?"

"No need to be formal. The name is Giles."

"That's a nice name. Are you from England? I ask because the only person I knew with that name was the character on Buffy the Vampire Slayer." Teagan said with a chuckle as she poured a healthy two fingers' worth of scotch into a tumbler.

"Ah, yes. Well, at least those vamps weren't glittery." He matched her chuckle.

"Very true." She took a sip of the scotch, and it slid down her throat smoothly. The bottle of scotch probably cost as much as her dress.

Damn you, Brooks.

"How do you like working for Mr. Bradley?"

She asked this because now that Brooks had completely undressed her soul by ironically dressing her up, she needed the lowdown of exactly what she was getting into with this boss.

"We don't talk a lot, but he seems nice. How about you?"

So much for getting the lowdown.

"Oh, I'm new. I actually start tomorrow. Mr. Bradley is taking me out for a business dinner to review my contract."

"That's nice of him. I think you are the first executive he's ever done that with."

"Really?" She put the glass back to her lips, and it was then that she realized she had nearly finished with the drink.

How did that happen?

The limo stopped completely, and the driver got out and opened the door for Teagan. She placed the glass on the bar and got out of the limo. As she stepped out, a hand gently guided her, and it belonged to Brooks.

"Brooks? Were you waiting for me outside the restaurant?"

"No. I just pulled in myself." He said with a smile as he tucked her hand around his arm.

"I guess this was perfect timing, then." She said to him as she moved her hand a bit until it rested around his arm.

It brushed his upper arm, which was rock-hard to the touch. Teagan's cheeks reddened as she thought about copping a generous feel of his ribcage. The man clearly worked out and was good at worshipping his body—too damned good. Her thoughts went south as images of straddling his waist and playing a tune over his washboard abs came over her.

Stop it, Teagan! He's your boss!

A sudden shudder came over her body as she imagined riding his cock.

Down, girl! Again, he's your boss! And you swore off men—remember?

"Have you ever been to L'Appart before?" He was smirking as he asked.

Damn it! Clearly, he reads minds. I am so fucked!

"Can't say that I have. Most places I go to have a menu above the register." She giggled as she said it, trying to recover from his smirk. He smiled brightly as he opened the door and escorted her into the restaurant.

"Well, looks like we are about to change that."

He locked his eyes on her. His eyes turned from a cool blue to a steely grey within seconds of telling her that. She swore she saw them do that during the interview, too. And as quickly as before, the steely grey was gone.

"Um, yeah. I guess so."

They walked up to a man, who immediately grabbed some menus and led them to a private table off the main dining area. It became apparent to Teagan that Mr. Bradley did not need to introduce himself anywhere.

Brooks pulled out the chair for Teagan as the man placed the menus on the corner side of the long table. He then removed the extra glassware and place settings.

"I trust you already have a wine selected for this evening, Mr. Bradley?"

"Yes, and there is no need for us to glance at the menu, Nico. We will go with a tasting each. And please start us off with? I'm sorry?" Brooks's eyes turned towards Teagan's. "Do you like Bourdeaux?"

"Are you kidding? That is my favorite kind of red wine!"

Shit! Is he reading my mind again, or is this a genuine question?

Before she could process anything, he smiled at the man and ordered.

"Outstanding. We will have the Château Gazin

Pomerol, Bordeaux, France 1989, to start with. Thanks, Nico. I'm not one for starting out with your pairings because that Bordeaux is my favorite--you know that." Brooks said with a smile as he passed the menus back to the man. His beard scrunched upright as he smiled. "Certainly, Mr. Bradley. Would you like pairings with the meal, though?"

"Please."

He took the menus and returned to the kitchen.

Teagan bit her lip before responding. She'd been with controlling asses that ordered for her before, but he asked about the wine, making her curious why he didn't let her look at the menu.

"So what's a tasting all about? I mean, you asked what kind of wine I like, and that's great! But I've never been comfortable with a guy ordering my food for me on a date."

Crap!

"And need I remind you, this is a business meeting, not a date?"

Brooks's eyes widened slightly, and he swallowed before responding.

Maybe he can't read minds?

"I'm sorry. I probably should have explained the menu process better before I had the chef walk off to get us the wine. A tasting is literally everything on the menu but in smaller portions. Nico's menu changes monthly, and I can't wait to see what he's prepared for this month. Forgive me for being so forward. You are right. This isn't a date—not that it would excuse the behavior, either. It's just," he swallowed again, but this time she noticed his Adam's apple enlarge before he continued, "I got excited. It's not every day I get to take someone to L'Appart that hasn't been. And truth be told, I want to see your bright eyes sparkle as you taste every delectable bite Nico offers. Will you forgive me for being such a jerk?"

Teagan bit her lip again as the words dripped from his soft, supple, sexy lips. Lips she envisioned kissing after his plight.

Stop this shit! He's your boss, Teagan!

"It's okay. It's just—after seeing the dress and everything else you picked out—" Teagan's voice trailed as her mouth suddenly went dry. She took a sip of water before continuing. "I just was in shock, and when you ordered, it made things seem weirder. But? What you ordered for me sounds wonderful."

"It wasn't hard to find out your sizes. You realize I own a lot of real estate—correct? The hotel you are staying in is one of mine, and I had management look at the sizes in your closet."

Well, that mystery is solved. At least Brooks can't read my mind. Phew!

"By the way, I'm a big eater, so please don't judge me, as I will probably not leave anything on my plate for leftovers."

"Given your size, I figured you for a salad eater, but I'm glad you have a hearty appetite. I do as well." He smiled brightly.

"Well, my father always told me I could pack it in,"

Teagan said while patting her stomach. She then blinked and swallowed hard. "But that's probably not what you want to hear. Should we discuss the contract? By the way, I signed the initial. It's always been normal to do that—well—at least I hope it is. Jeremy, my first boss out of college, made me sign the first one, and then we added addendums to it."

Brooks's eyes darkened as she uttered Jeremy's name.

"Your former boss had you do something like that?"

"Well, yeah. Jeremy said that was customary. It was my first real job, and I assumed that was the norm when Jeremy took over his father's company."

"It's not the norm."

Teagan noticed Brooks's jaw clench. A flashback of earlier in the afternoon rushed her thoughts.

"Mr. Bradley, I'm sorry. I didn't mean to upset you." She said as she patted the back of his hand.

His emotional anger went from zero to sixty in five seconds flat, and Teagan wasn't sure why. What did her former boss's fuck up have to do with Brooks's mood, anyway? It was all so strange. But even stranger was how she calmed him just as quickly as his nostrils had flared moments ago. Brooks's jaw softened as she continued to pat his hand. That could only mean one thing. He was attracted to her.

Shit! I'm so fucked!

"No, I'm sorry. It's just I get mad when I hear people being taken advantage of. You shouldn't have signed the initial agreement. In fact," He started as he pulled out his cell phone. "I'm going to text Anne now so she can destroy the original document you signed."

Teagan let in a breath through her gaping mouth.

"Wait! I'm sorry! I didn't mean for you to text her. God! I didn't even start this job, and I'm already causing so many problems!"

Brooks put down his cell and locked his eyes on Teagan's.

"Teagan, no. You aren't causing problems at all. I'm only angered that an employer put you in that kind of vulnerable position. He took advantage of your kindness, and that isn't right."

Teagan scoffed before responding.

"Yeah, well, he wasn't just an employer." Her eyes widened once she realized what she had said. "Oh my God, I'm sorry! That was TMI, wasn't it? You don't need to know about my ex. This isn't a date, after all." She swallowed hard and then bit her lip.

Why does this guy always make me want to spill my guts? I've never been this honest with anyone ever before. Not a friend, a lover, and certainly not someone I'm employed with!

"If you are implying that he was your boyfriend, that makes his indiscretion with you so much worse. I'm very sorry he took advantage of you."

"Actually, he was my fiancé up until a few days ago. I caught him cheating on me with his personal secretary."

Brooks's jaw visibly tightened again.

Why would he do that? This is just a business dinner—right?

"He should have never done that to you."

"Well, I got even—sort of. I hit the ass with a stapler."

Brooks let out a chuckle at the same time as Teagan.

"I would have paid to see that! So, I take that you are staying at a hotel because you left the place you shared."

Teagan scoffed.

"More like he kicked me out. He somehow blamed me for everything and said there was no way I could afford the place because he was firing me. He and his slut put a restraining order on me, so technically, I wouldn't have been able to work there, anyway. No matter. I wouldn't have stayed under his employment. And frankly, I'm glad I'm rid of him. I thought I'd be more upset, but I haven't cried over him and his stupidity in quite some time. I guess things were over between us long before I hit him with his office supplies." Teagan chuckled again, but it was more out of embarrassment this time. She'd done it again. Revealed too much.

God damn it!

She crossed her arms and let out a breath before continuing.

"Speaking of being able to afford things," she uncrossed her arms and patted Brooks's forearm. To her surprise, the muscles were just as rock-hard as his upper arms. "Brooks, I know this outfit and the jewelry are expensive. I mean, I was considering insuring myself before I stepped out the door to get here. It's nice of you to do this, but it's too much."

"Teagan, I wanted to do this."

"But it's all so expensive. Even eating at this place will set you back a few grand. And it's just a business meeting—right?"

"Teagan, I'm a billionaire. Dropping a few grand will not break my bank account. Please, let me spoil you. And for the record, this doesn't need to be a business meeting. It can be a date if you'd like. From the sound of things, it appears you deserve to be doted on. And I'd be more than happy to be the lucky man to do that for you."

Teagan smiled slightly.

"There's no denying that I like you. I would, but that would be stupid on my part since I've already admitted earlier today that you are hot as hell. But I can only assume that you put that Christmas Clause in my contract for a reason. And I can't help but wonder if it's for a similar reason as mine for swearing off dating for a while. Did someone burn you?"

"Yes, but haven't we all been burned at one point or another?"

"I'm sure, but none of us like being a rebound, either."

"I can assure you that I'm over her. My clause had more to do with not wanting to get taken advantage of. I mean, I am a billionaire, after all. And many women I've dated in the past seem to think I should spend that money on them. You are the first woman I've met that doesn't seem to think so."

"Look, as my boss, I really think this is too much. And we are here to discuss the terms of my contract. So I say that there should be a budget for my wardrobe for the contract we agree upon. I'm not a Barbie doll, and I don't need the yellow van as an accessory—nor do I need the Dream Home."

"Fair enough. But this will not be a beer-budget type of thing, either. I pick the dollar amount for each occasion because white-tie affairs are extremely specific. And no woman on my arm will look lesser than a ten in the rags."

Teagan let out a breath.

"I can see you're going to give me an argument about this—aren't you?"

"I won't need to if you agree," Brooks said with a smirk that reached his eyes. Damn him. He then tucked a strand of hair behind Teagan's ear before continuing. "That dress is stunning, and it was worth every penny to see it on you. Now, getting back to the discussion about whether this is a date or business. What are your thoughts on that?"

Brooks's eyes flicked to Teagan's lips. Her body tingled with the mere action. She was sure her knees would buckle if she wasn't sitting down.

Why is he doing this to me? He's so hot, and if he kissed me right now, I wouldn't stop him. I'm so damned fucked.

"I'd say that this could be a date if—"

Brooks pressed his lips on hers before she could finish her sentence. But they broke the kiss once Nico came to the table with the wine. He poured a glass for each of them, and Brooks raised his glass.

"A toast! Here's to the start of a beautiful relationship." He touched his glass to Teagan's and took a sip.

"So about that whole Christmas Clause thing?" Teagan said as she took a sip of her own. The wine was dry and smooth on her tongue, just as she liked it. "What should we do about that?"

"Well, I think we will make a perfect pair this holiday season. What do you think?."

"Um, I think you aren't looking for a relationship, and neither am I at the moment. So we can go to these events as friends? That fits the Christmas Clause in the contract."

"True, but I've got this need to kiss you again, and that won't work with that Christmas Clause written the way it is." He said as he cupped her cheek.

"Well, you are the boss. Perhaps we should add an addendum to the contract?"

"I couldn't agree more." He drew his lips to hers. The kiss was sweet and soft. "It's settled. We will add an addendum, so I can kiss you whenever I want. In fact? Can we kiss on that instead of shaking hands?" He said with another smirk that reached his eyes.

Chapter Seven

"Wait—exactly what are you saying, Anne?"

"Her father was of Gaelic descent, and her mother was Italian and German."

"Okay, I still don't follow," Brooks said as he shook his head.

"The father was a kelpie, and the mother was a Strega from the Kersh clan, and somehow the mother is related to Alec Christianson." Said Anne with a determined look.

"That's a trifecta."

"Yes."

"You understand what this means—don't you?" Brooks said as he placed his hands on Anne's shoulders.

"Yes, she needs our protection now more than ever. Hybrids are not well-liked, thanks to Keme's proclamations in the past. She needs protection from the werewolves and the vampires."

"That's the understatement of the century. Werewolves were the ones that wrote the law, saying hybrids were a freak of nature. No intermixing of magical bloodlines is allowed. But I don't see any of a shifter's basic qualities in her. She doesn't have the aura. Aside from her appetite and scent, little else would clue me in on her being a shifter."

"Her witch side must be suppressing her shifter side somehow."

"Do Raine and Skye know? I can't picture them not protecting their kin—even if they are distant cousins."

"I don't think they know about her. In fact, it was hard gaining the little information I could on her. I'll refer to my grimoire for more information about how she could suppress her shifter side. The wolves nearly killed off all known hybrids in the New England area when Lenox murdered Rogan. So there isn't much on the subject, but my grandmother wrote what she knew."

"Okay, good."

"How are you going to keep her under your protection? I mean, she will eventually go home after her workday is done."

"For now, I'll make up as many excuses as I can to keep her with me, whether planning for the upcoming gala or a food tasting. And the coven can patrol the condo complex until I buy that property and move into the vacant condo next to hers. She'll be safe at the hotel since I already own it and the clan has orders to patrol the area as of right now." Brooks said as he fired off a text.

"Do you really think you can become her neighbor? Don't you think she'd get a little suspicious about that?"

"Do you have any better ideas?"

"No, I guess not."

"Now go appear to be busy. Teagan will be entering the office any minute, according to Damon."

"How'd he get the morning detail?"

"The others pulled a double shift on last night's patrol because Tyler is back in the city."

"The last thing we need is for that werewolf to put two and two together with Teagan, Brooks!"

"Exactly. Now please make the appropriate calls so I can acquire Macklowe Properties and Compass Development on One Wall Street. They are in a bit of a standstill with the construction because of Covid, so supposedly, they are eager for a quick sale."

"She's coming," Anne said in a whisper. She

cleared her throat before continuing. "Will do, Mr. Bradley."

As Anne turned to leave, Teagan walked into Brooks's office.

"I hope I'm not interrupting anything important. I can come back if you need me to." Teagan said as she waved her hand towards the door.

"I was just leaving. He's all yours." Anne said as she walked by her and headed toward her office.

Teagan turned to Brooks.

"So, boss, what's on the agenda for today?"

"We've got some party planning during the day and a tasting to do this evening for the gala."

"Okay? So I'm guessing this is going to be a long day?"

"Most likely, yes."

Tonight would be the full moon, and that worried Brooks. Shifters didn't really need the moon to shift, but all shifters could draw on its power, strengthening them during a full moon. He had to find a way to ask her if she was a hybrid, but that wouldn't be easy. No hybrid would trust a vampire or were after the wolves killed most of them. He had to gain her trust so she'd tell him her secret.

Chapter Eight

The morning went by quickly in the office, with Teagan taking notes and offering ideas for fun games to play during the holiday gala event. It was nearly two when Brooks peered at his watch.

"Let's grab a quick coffee and then head to The Plaza for some prep and the tasting." He said as he reached for his jacket draped across his chair.

"Sounds good to me. I need a little pick me up, or I'll fall asleep on you during the tasting."

They headed to the elevator and down to the

lobby, where the limo met them. Giles opened the door, and they both got in.

"Would you like a drink? I usually only stock this with scotch, but I might've stashed a bottle of wine in here somewhere."

"A scotch is fine," Teagan said with a smile.

Brooks poured two tumblers with a shot in each of them and handed one to Teagan.

"Hopefully, the boss is okay with us drinking on the job," Teagan chuckled.

"The boss and I are tight, and he won't mind," Brooks said with a wink. "And besides, I'm basically keeping you after hours for a tasting, so it's not like we are on the proverbial clock."

"True. So, what's this tasting all about? Are we picking things based on the theme of the gala?"

"The theme for this year is silver bells. I'm not sure how close to the theme we can get with the food without it being gross."

Brooks chuckled again.

"Yeah, I'm not in the mood for anything metallic in taste, but we could center the food choices around the shape of a bell. For instance, a pear is sort of bell-shaped, and there are a lot of delicious dishes made with pears. Cocktail shrimp served on silver platters would also work, and coconut shrimp would work with the theme, too. Oh! And what about cupcakes and cookies with silver and white accents?"

Brooks smiled brightly.

"I knew I hired the right person for this job. You are a natural at this."

Teagan shrugged.

"It's not terribly difficult to plan a gala once we've already set the theme. I've done my fair share of planning events like these."

"Well, it all sounds perfect to me. I'm sure The Plaza planned a set of choices for the menu, but with your ideas, we can pick some great ones to go with the theme."

The limo came to a stop, and they got out. Brooks offered his arm, and Teagan gladly took it as he walked towards the entrance. Brook opened the door and led her through it to the main entrance.

As they walked into The Plaza, Brooks's jaw tightened as a man approached them. He was just as tall and muscular as Brooks, but he had sandy blond hair as opposed to Brooks's dark hair.

"Brooks! It's been a while." The man said as he outstretched his hand towards Brooks.

"Yes, it has been a while, Tyler. What brings you to the city?"

"I'm here on business," Tyler said, as his eyes shifted from Brooks over to Teagan's.

"And you are?"

"Teagan Thompson. I work for Mr. Bradley." Teagan said as she outstretched her hand.

Tyler took her hand and drew the back of it to his lips.

"It's a pleasure meeting you, Ms. Thompson. I hope my brother is treating you well."

"We are not, nor have we ever been, brothers by blood, Tyler," Brooks said in a low growl.

"Watch your mouth, brother. You might scare off the little lady with your razor tongue."

"What are you really doing here, Tyler?"

"Let's get a drink over at the bar—shall we?"

"I have a business meeting to attend right now. I can't meet you for a drink, Tyler—not that I'd ever want to."

Tyler grabbed Brooks's forearm and whispered in Brooks's ear. The words were only audible for Brooks.

"You will have a drink with me before you leave The Plaza, or I will snap your hybrid pet Teagan's neck before you have time to react."

"Teagan, why don't you go on in for the tasting, and I'll catch up with you? This won't take long."

"Sure. I'll take notes so we can decide on everything once you return. It was nice meeting you, Tyler." Teagan said with a smile as she turned on her heel and headed towards one of the meeting rooms.

Brooks waited until she was out of earshot before responding to Tyler.

"What are you talking about? Teagan is no hybrid! She's my executive administrative assistant."

Tyler smiled and led Brooks to the hotel bar, where he ordered two scotches and handed one to Brooks.

"Your coven better use a little more discretion when they tail me. I spotted Damon from a mile away.

His stench is extremely recognizable. Once I detected him and who he was protecting, I did some digging. Your little personal assistant pet is born of kelpie and Strega witch blood. She's also related to Alec Christianson, King of the Vlad Coven Clan. Therefore, she's a hybrid and an abomination by definition. And since it's against The Common Trifecta Law to intermix magical bloodlines, I will kill her while you watch."

"Okay, first, she's no shifter. Her aura is clear, and you should have known that the minute you shook her hand. Second, you wouldn't be stupid enough to try that here. There are too many innocents in this hotel. You'll risk exposure."

"Oh, Brooks, you may only be my adoptive brother, so I can't fault you for your genes. But you can be so stupid sometimes. I have this place surrounded by my pack. The two of you won't make it across the street." Tyler said as he took the last swig of his scotch. He patted Brooks on the shoulder and walked out of the bar.

Shit!

Brooks mumbled a few other choice words as he took out his cell phone and texted Damon.

Tyler is at The Plaza. I need the coven here.

Please make arrangements with Plaza management for me to have the penthouse this evening.

He then texted Anne.

Tyler knows about Teagan. You'll have to work fast to uncover the truth about her. I'll stay

at The Plaza tonight with Teagan to keep her safe.

Also, inform Giles and see if he can enlist the help of Steffen and the rest of our neighboring coven in Albany, NY.

It was a few seconds before each of them texted back with a "will do." That put him at ease slightly, but Tyler was still a threat to them. It wasn't like he could follow Teagan to the bathroom—that would be too suspicious. He rushed to the meeting room and found Teagan with Tyler. A pit formed deep within his stomach.

"Brooks! Thanks for covering the tab back at the bar. Teagan and I were having a great conversation and getting to know one another. Did you know her mother was of Strega descent, and her father was Gaelic? I find that extremely fascinating. Don't you?"

"Teagan is a new hire. I planned this tasting so we could get better acquainted. I'm sure you understand this is a team-building exercise, Tyler, and I need you to leave."

"How rude of me! Of course! Perhaps we can bump into each other later. I'd love another drink so we can all get acquainted." Tyler said with a wink as he sauntered off towards the lobby of The Plaza.

"Sorry, it took me a bit. How is the tasting going so far?"

"It's going pretty well! They had some pear dishes on the salad menu, and I made notes for the ones I preferred. We are going to start the main course next, so you are just in time."

A few beeps from Brooks's phone broke the conversation. He peered at the message from Anne.

I'll be there shortly with an herbal extract you can slip in her wine. It's made of comfrey, an herb to heal wounds, and valerian, to make her drowsy so you can get her to the penthouse. It also contains rose water, which purifies her blood.

She needs to drink it. The spell I've placed over the elixir will keep her alive. A werewolf's bite can't kill her so long as she drinks this tonic.

Brooks responded with two short words back.

Thank you.

Brooks immediately looked up from his phone after the texts from Anne.

"I'm very sorry. Anne is rewriting your contract terms and has questions about the wording. Forgive me. I don't like to ignore the people in front of me because of the business on my phone. How about we have a glass of wine with our tastings? I'm sure I can get the server to bring us a bottle."

Teagan smiled.

"Actually, that's not a bad idea. They have served no alcohol yet, and I think it will be important for us to suggest pairings at the gala—don't you?"

"I couldn't agree more."

He hailed down a familiar face among the servers. It was Damon who was pretending to be a member of the staff at the tasting. Damon, Brooks's right hand, immediately came over. His dark eyes and hair appeared to be just as strong as his personality and stature as he towered over the table.

"Good evening! My name is Damon. What can I help you both with?"

"It's nice to meet you again, Damon! Brooks mentioned that we should have some sample suggestions from the wines for our gala. Would you mind bringing over some flutes?"

Damon smiled brightly at Teagan before answering.

"Actually, we are serving full bottles, and I'll bring over the first choice shortly." He said as he eyed Brooks.

Brooks nodded, a mutual understanding shared between them.

Anne is coming with the elixir, Damon. Meet her in the kitchen.

Will do, boss. Anything else besides circling the perimeter tonight?

No. That will be all. Teagan will be staying with me in the Grand Penthouse, the one on the north side of the building.

Gonna get frisky?

Damon! Stop!

Just kidding, boss. I know it's a two-bedroom suite, and you are a gentleman, but you aren't fooling anyone. You have feelings for the woman.

That's enough, Damon. Get the elixir now.

Brooks smiled at Damon as Damon turned on his

heel to head to the kitchen to wait for Anne. Once he opened the kitchen doors, Anne appeared.

"Where's the bottle?"

"It's right here," Damon said as he handed it over. "But how will you get that elixir into the bottle without me opening it? You understand that I have to open the bottle in front of them, so Teagan doesn't get suspicious."

"Clearly, you've never seen a witch perform magic!" Anne said with a smile.

Anne waved her hand over the mortar and pestle containing the herbs and another hand over the rose water. They all floated in the air and magically entered the bottle. Once inside, Anne waved her hands again, and the wine began stirring inside the bottle on its own, diluting the herbs into the bottle and making them disappear. She handed the bottle to Damon, who headed to Brooks and Teagan.

Damon opened the bottle and poured two glasses, and served them both. Brooks raised his glass to Teagan.

"Here's to a successful gala." Their glasses clinked, and Teagan took a sip. Brooks smiled and sighed. A warmth washed over him that Teagan would be safe from the bite of a werewolf. But he'd have to kill Tyler to keep her truly safe. No one can find out the truth about Teagan, or she'll have a target on her back for the rest of her life.

Teagan finished her glass and yawned repeatedly.

"Brooks, I'm sorry. I don't know why, but I'm suddenly very sleepy. I think I should head home."

"Certainly, I'll text Giles to bring the car to the front."

Teagan nodded off the instant he took his phone out of his pocket. Damon slipped Brooks the hotel key card, and Brooks brought Teagan up to the penthouse and laid her on one of the beds before the drowsy portion of the elixir wore off.

Chapter Nine

"Brooks, what happened? Did I fall asleep on you?" Teagan said as she sat up and pulled the covers away.

"That you did."

She peered around the unfamiliar room with knitted brows. "Where are we?"

"The penthouse suite at The Plaza. I brought you here because I didn't have the heart to wake you. But that really isn't important right now. Teagan, there's something I've been trying to talk to you about for a while now. And it never seemed to be the right time.

But now you are in danger, and we must talk about your lineage."

"Um, okay. What is it?"

"First off, don't be frightened." His voice was soft as he pulled her into his lap. "I would never hurt you, Teagan. Please know that before we go any further."

She palmed his cheek. "I trust you, Brooks."

"Good. So there's no easy way to say this, so I'm just going to come right out with it. Your mother, a distant cousin of Alec Christianson, the King of the Vlad Vampire clan, was also a Strega witch. That combination would have been fine, but your father was a kelpie shifter. You are a trifecta, and that makes you a hybrid. Tyler is a werewolf, and he is trying to kill you because—"

"Because I'm a supposed abomination. Yeah. I know the story." Teagan began to shake. "I was told to hide myself from all magical beings because they wouldn't understand me. My kelpie father fell in love with my mother, who had a powerful bloodline to begin with. With the trifecta, they had the first female kelpie shifter in existence. Me. All of them were male before I came along. After some research, they discovered that my mother's magic was why I'm a female, not a male kelpie shifter. Somehow, her magic was the catalyst—but? Magic has a funny way of balancing itself out. Normally because I'm a shifter, a werewolf bite wouldn't kill me. But since I also have vampire blood, a werewolf bite is lethal. How did you figure all this out? I've been cloaking my shifter aura since my father died.

Apparently, my mother, before her death, linked him and me with her magic to keep me safe. Once he died, the spell broke, and I shifted into my black horse. That's how I discovered my suppressed shifter side's existence."

"That makes sense because, as a vampire, I shouldn't have been able to figure out your shifter side so easily with your magical barrier. You may have been cloaking your shifter side, but there's one thing you can't cloak from any magical being."

"I read my mother's grimoire and did the spell perfectly, so I don't understand how you figured it out. The only way for me to be detected by another magical being is if they are my mate."

Brooks sucked in a breath and nodded.

"Yeah, exactly. That's the one thing you can't hide from. I had suspicions because I could sense your beautiful, distinct shifter scent. But you masking your aura threw both Anne and myself off. I had Anne research you and your family; by then, it was easy to put two and two together."

"Wait, so we are mates? Really?"

"It would appear so."

"And I know Tyler's a werewolf. I gathered that when he introduced himself, I could see his aura."

"My coven and I will keep you safe from Tyler. I promise he won't harm you."

"I have to leave town, Brooks. He won't stop coming after me, and I don't want you or your coven hurt because of me. Trust me when I say this is a fight you don't want to get involved with. That law means everything to the wolves. They will stop at nothing to destroy me. Hell—they nearly killed Alec for dating a werewitch. They weren't even serious at the time. And now? Morgan's witch powers lie dormant. Their potential offspring are no more dangerous than I am." Teagan said as she lowered her feet to the floor. "I appreciate you trying to keep me safe, but the only way I will be is if I put enough distance between Tyler and me because his bite will kill me."

"That's where you are wrong. The wine you had at dinner contained an elixir that Anne had made, and it purified your blood. He can't kill you with his bite any longer."

"Well, thank you both, but I can't have you helping me. This isn't your fight. I'd be heartbroken if either of you got hurt. The werewolves will kill you because you are sympathetic toward a hybrid. And what's worse? This could start another Civil Were War."

"Teagan, no. Tyler made it my fight when he threatened you. You are a kelpie, and you, out of any other shifter race, can appreciate that a mate bond is the strongest bond in existence. I can't just shut off my need to protect you. That's impossible." Brooks said as he tucked a piece of hair behind Teagan's ear.

"I understand that because I want to go to keep you safe. But I'm finding it awfully hard to stay away from you, and I'm also finding it hard to keep arguing with you."

"Good, then you'll stay."

Brooks cupped her cheek and drew her lips towards his. The kiss was just as soft and sweet as their first. But it grew needy when he parted her lips to deepen the kiss.

"I've wanted to kiss you like this since I first met you."

Teagan smiled and cupped his cheek.

"I have, too."

"Well, now that I know you won't be fighting me for keeping you safe, how about we order some room service? I think both you and I could use a drink since our evening was cut short. How about a bottle of red?"

"That sounds good. While you order, I will find a movie for us to watch."

"Okay."

Brooks called downstairs for room service, returned to the bedroom, and sat next to Teagan. She turned to him and smiled.

"I still can't get over the fact that we are fated mates. It's so surreal to me. I've heard about shifters falling in love at first sight, but I never dreamed it would happen to me—and with a vampire, no less."

"I'm happy we found each other. Christmas will be much brighter now that you are in my life."

He pulled her close to him and claimed her lips.

"I want you, Teagan." He whispered over her lips.

"I want you, too."

He caressed her hair as his lips slid from her mouth to her neck. She let out a soft moan as he settled his lips on the crux of her neck. His hands slid down the length of her body before settling at her waist.

"I want to kiss every inch of you, Teagan."

His lips trailed from her neck and down the length of her body. He shimmied her black pencil skirt to her hips and slid off her black lace thong panties.

"I need to taste you, Teagan," Brooks said as he teased her clit with his skillful tongue. "God, you are so wet." He plunged a couple of fingers inside her.

She writhed beneath him, arching her back to give him better access to her perfect pussy. She bunched the sheets in her fists, signifying she was about to go over the edge. He smiled as he watched her hooded gaze lock onto him.

"Baby, please. I need you."

"Then you shall have me." He said as he removed their clothing and plunged inside her slick center.

She cupped his ass pulling his waist closer to her with each one of his thrusts.

"God, baby, you feel so good wrapped around my dick."

Her mouth formed the most perfect *o* as the sweetest, sexiest sounds came from her lips. Moan after glorious moan filled the room with each of his thrusts.

"That's it, baby. Let yourself go. Come for me."

Just as his command left his lips, she obliged as her perfect pussy pulsated around his cock, causing him to fill her with his own sweet release. After they cleaned up in the shower, there was a knock at the door.

"The wine must be here. You sit tight. I'll get it." He said with a wink before leaving the room.

Brooks headed down the hallway and was in complete bliss. In all of his years of existence, he'd never felt this connected to a woman before. With a smile on his face and no care in the world except for the blonde beauty in his bed, Brooks opened the door without peering into the peephole. It was a mistake because he came face-to-face with Tyler at the threshold of his door.

Fuck!

"Tyler!"

Teagan heard the name ring through the penthouse and leaped off the bed to lock the bedroom door. Just hearing the name sent a chill down her spine, leaving her almost frozen with fear. But her mate was out there with Tyler, and the need to protect Brooks outweighed her lifetime of fears of being killed for who she was. She needed to shift into her horse, and now.

"You should have picked a less conspicuous room, Brooks. The penthouse is so predictable." Tyler said as he placed the bottle of wine on the credenza and walked in.

"Call me crazy, but the penthouse is supposed to keep out the riffraff like you," Brooks said as his fangs lengthened.

Tyler was shifting into his wolf as Brooks connected his fist with Tyler's jaw.

"You won't hurt her. I'll kill you first."

"I'd like to see you try, Brooks."

The two rolled around on the floor, swiping, biting, and growling. Teagan opened the bedroom door and then shifted into her horse. Once she made it into the penthouse's living area, she saw Tyler over Brooks with a paw ready to strike. Teagan lunged at Tyler and then bucked him, sending Tyler across the room. His head hit the cascading quartz of the bar. A thunderous crack whipped through the room as soon as his head made contact with the hard stone. Tyler let out a whimper before shifting back to his human half.

Brooks quickly ran towards the heap that was Tyler on the floor. He checked for a pulse but couldn't find one.

"He's dead, baby. He can't hurt you anymore."

Teagan shifted back into her human half and rushed into Brooks's arms.

"Thank you for saving me."

Brooks cupped her face and kissed her forehead.

"I think I should be thanking you. After all, you were the one that killed Tyler by flinging him across the room."

"Yes, but you fought him until I could shift into my kelpie."

Brooks drew her forehead to his. "I will always protect you, baby. Always. Now let me text the coven so they can get that carcass out of here. We don't need to risk exposure with the humans."

Teagan smiled, grabbed the bottle of wine, and

opened it. She poured out two heavy-handed glasses and handed one to Brooks.

"I think we can definitely use this drink now."

"I think you are right," Brooks said as he connected his glass to hers. The clinking sound filled the room.

THREE WEEKS HAD PASSED SINCE THE DEATH of Tyler, and all was quiet. It was now apparent that Tyler had taken Teagan's secret to his grave. Still, she continued to cloak her shifter side from all other magical beings just to be safe. Eventually, she'd have to contact Alec, Raine, and Skye to help convince the shifter council that she was not a threat to humanity. All magic has its limits, and her mother's grimoire had proof. But that was a battle for another day. Right now? All Teagan wanted to do was enjoy her freedom. For so many years, she'd felt like she was in the human Witness Protection Program, hiding her identity out of fear for her life. And now she didn't need to do that.

In fact, all Teagan had to focus on was getting the hang of her new position at Bradley Corp as Vice President. Brooks promoted her the minute they became an item, and Teagan couldn't be happier with the outcome. She thought she had her dream job right out of college, but this one hit her life goals right out of the ballpark!

She was about to head out of the office to the gala ball she and Brooks had planned since their tasting. Giles drove her to The Plaza, and Teagan walked into the main lobby, where Brooks greeted her.

"I'm glad you are here. I was starting to worry that you'd run late." Brooks said with a nervous laugh. It wasn't like him to be nervous, making her brows knit.

"Well, you said not to be late, so here I am. But? Is everything okay? You don't seem like yourself."

"I'm wonderful! Let's get a drink before we head into the ballroom."

He still seemed off, but Teagan shook her head and smiled as Brooks led her to the bar area. The bartender brought over a bottle of champagne and two empty fluted glasses. The one he handed Teagan contained a diamond ring. Teagan's eyes lit up, and she palmed her chest.

"Teagan, ever since you walked into my life, I've learned to laugh and to love again. You've made me so, so happy, and I never want a day to go by without your light in it. Will you marry me?"

Teagan cupped her mouth. Tears dotted the corners of her eyes before a steady stream flowed down her cheeks.

"Oh, Brooks. Yes! I will marry you!"

He placed the ring on her finger and kissed Teagan's forehead.

"I love you with all of my heart, my future Mrs. Teagan Bradley. Merry Christmas."

"And I love you too. Your love is the best Christmas gift you could ever give me."

The End

Before You Go...

Want to know when my next story will come out? Join my newsletter!

https://www.authoramandakimberley.com/news letter-signup

About the Author

AMANDA KIMBERLEY

USA TODAY BESTSELLING
AUTHOR

USA Today Best Selling and award winning author Amanda Kimberley has written in various genres in the course of almost four decades.

Her nonfiction blog, which focuses on the chronic disease fibromyalgia, has garnered recognition from various organizations, including Health Magazine. Naming her blog, Fibro and Fabulous, as a top blog for fibro sufferers.

Amanda has also written for medical magazines

and sites like FM Aware, The National Fibromyalgia Association's magazine and ProHealth.

When Kimberley is not writing nonfiction, she enjoys penning romance. Her first Furry United Coalition story, The Turtle and the Hare, earned the 2020 Summer Splash Book Awards of Ink and Scratches for Best Romance. Her Forever Series Books, Forever Friends and Forever Bound were featured in 2015 and 2016 on the BookCountry website, a division of Penguin/Random House as editor's picks. She has also been featured as a USA Today Happy Ever After Hot List Indie Author with Claiming My Valentine, a Best Poet of the 90's ranking for an anthology, and has had a #1 PNR ranking with Immortal Hunger and Hearts Unleashed.

Amanda Kimberley is a Connecticut native that now lives in the warmth of Northern Texas with her zoo consisting of her husky, tuxedo cat, mice, rabbits, guinea pigs, a tank of fish, two daughters, and a husband.

When she is not writing you can find her cooking whole foods for her pack. She also enjoys reading, hiking, and gaming.

facebook.com/authoramandakimberley

twitter.com/KimberleyLB

instagram.com/amandakimberleylb

bookbub.com/profile/amanda-kimberley

Also by Amanda Kimberley

Forever Loved

(Coming Soon)

Forever Yours

(Coming Soon)

Forever Mine

(Coming Soon)

Historical PNR Series
The Witch Journals Series

Salem's Trial by Judge

Salem's Trial by Township

Salem's Trial by Birth

(Coming Soon)

The Gypsy Witch Trials

(Coming Soon)

Colonial Witch Trials

(Coming Soon)

Stand Alone PNR

The Cure

Manifestations

Uncharted

The Pride Within

Co-Author Stand-Alone PNR

By the Pool with Alex Kimberley

Scifi Fantasy PNR
Suburban Shifter & Celestials Series

Loving the Alpha

Loving the Lion

(Coming Soon)

Loving the Legacy

(Coming Soon)

Loving the Original

(Coming Soon)

Loving the Lone Wolf

(Coming Soon)

Loving the Rogue

(Coming Soon)

The Pandemic Series

Pandemic Passion

Pandemic Pandemonium

(Coming Soon)

The Season of Shifters Series

Midnight & Mistletoe

Midnight & Magic

(Coming Soon)

Midnight & Memories

(Coming Soon)

RomCom PNR

The Eve L. Worlds Hellenic Island Shifter Series

The Turtle and the Hare

The Turtle and the Rock

The Ferret and the Fossa

(Coming Soon)

Contemporary Romance

The Chronic Collection

Down by the Willow Tree

To Hell With Carpets

Welcome Home

The Chronic Collection

The Just Series

Just Breathe

Just Believe

(Coming Soon)

Just Be

(Coming Soon)

Nonfiction Self Help

The Fibro and Fabulous Series

Fibro and Fabulous: The Book

Fibromyalgia and Sex Can Be a Pain in the Neck

Fibromyalgia and Pregnancy

Poetry

Blue Water Baptism

The Puzzle Called Life

If You Liked Midnight & Mergers Then You Might Like...

EQUIPOISE
SOLAR
SYSTEM
SERIES

Laying
Claim
to the
Lion

USA TODAY BEST SELLING AUTHOR
AMANDA
KIMBERLEY

Laying Claim to the Lion

CHAPTER ONE

"This isn't an option, Verena. If you don't want to marry, you have no choice but to find a suitable male to conceive an heir. Jaxson saw to it that the Valet de Chambre isn't in our favor. And after the Battle of Quell, we appear weak."

Tilda stroked Verena's chestnut hair to braid it. She formed four strands to make a sizeable French braid with Verena's dark locks.

"So what do you expect me to do, Tilda? It's not like our planet has any males on it! And with Jaxson taking over almost all the Equipoise solar system, I won't find anyone willing to defy him."

Verena sighed as she turned to meet Tilda's gaze.

"You certainly can't give into Jaxson. He may want you as his queen, but you know mating with him will be a certain sentence to slavery. Not to mention what it will mean for the rest of our pride. We've always had an option to seek a mate from any planet of our choosing.

But if Jaxson gets his way, none of them are safe. We will be forced to only mate with the people of Emir." Said Tilda.

"I would never think of giving in to him. That panther is simply barbaric! But finding a mate who isn't under Jaxson's tyranny will be hard."

"Earth would be your best option. That solar system is several galaxies away and has never heard of Jaxson. But you must be careful there. Many of the humans on Earth can not shift, and what's worse is that most of them do not believe in shifters. The people are primitive, but if you stick to your feminity, you will find a mate in enough time."

Verena frowned and gripped the guild-colored arm of her thrown. She massaged the lion-carved paw that protruded and curled around the bottom of the arm, hoping the gesture would allow her the privilege of perspective.

"Verena, there are some shifters on that planet, and your abilities will allow you to sense they are. However, they are not as advanced as us. Many of the men are as barbaric as Jaxson. Very possessive, very domineering. But some are suitable mates for an heir."

Tilda shrugged her shoulders and peered out the large glass window that overlooked the lush kingdom. Her eyes fixed on the rainforest that was a little past the main village. A rainbow was forming, and Tilda smiled. That seemed like a good omen, but she also always loved to meditate on them. And with Effeminate's future hanging in the balance, she could use all the meditating she could find.

"That wasn't what was really bothering me. Shifter or not, it really doesn't matter. I just need the man's seed. I'm not going there to find a mate. The Valet de Chambre's decree merely states that we need an heir. Therefore, I don't need to bring home a mate."

Tilda blinked a few times and then gazed into Verena's eyes.

"What do you mean, you aren't going there to find a mate? We need a king. A king will protect us from Jaxson's tyranny."

Verena stood up and narrowed her eyes as she gazed at Tilda and walked past her towards the window. She placed her hands on the sill and looked out at the vast green jungle, farmlands, and stone buildings that made up the planet she had loved and cared for since birth. Verena pointed out toward the stone-engineered buildings that looked like the pyramids of Earth they once helped the Egyptians build.

"Look at all of them. These women are brilliant and strong. They do not need any male to help protect them, nor do they need a male to construct a building for them. We women of Effeminate built a foundation of powerful warriors in our own right, and I will not let one battle determine our downfall."

"Verena, it may have only been one battle, but it was one that killed your parents and extended this war into several hundred cycles. There's also no end in sight. As your general, I think it's wise for us to explore other options to end it. Especially now that the panther shifters have taken over all but two planets in our solar system. It's just us and the planet Tatsu who are not under Jaxson's thumb."

"Jaxson will never overthrow the dragon shifters. He's not powerful enough to defeat Dragon Jilocasin of Tatsu."

"True, but it is only a matter of time where even the Tatsus will be against us. It's not like those over-grown reptiles have been friendly with any warm-blooded cat ever before. None of the treaties apply to them because of how cold-blooded they are. They don't practice diplomacy. All they seem to do is produce law as part of the council without seeing first-hand how that law will affect any planet. No, the only way to fight off Jaxson is if we find some alphas to help us defeat him. Planet Emir won't have a chance against the shifter species of Earth. I just know it. And besides, your own mother believed in the value of having a male mate from the planet Earth. Having a partner gives you perspective when leading your great people."

Tilda placed her hand on Verena's shoulder. Verena brushed it off.

"Yes, and look at what that value got her! She's dead, Tilda, and so is my father! I can do nothing about that except fight Jaxson without showing weak-ness. And I believe my father was my mother's down-fall. Her love for him was why she fell in battle." Verena crossed her arms and shook her head before continuing, "Her head was too clouded with love.

That's why she didn't see that panther coming for her. She was so fixated on the one killing my father. No! I will not allow our sisters to be clouded with love, fear, or apprehension. They don't need to be tied down to a man. They need to focus on this war. We will win the Ebb War and in honor of my mother!" Verena clenched fists. "Now, please prepare my ship for my solo trip to Earth."

"You don't plan on having an escort?"

"What do I need protection from, Tilda? You said it yourself. These shifters are primitive compared to us. I shouldn't need any help with them or finding a suitable seed."

"Yes, my Queen," Tilda bowed before continuing. "How long do you plan on staying so I can better prepare your wardrobe and rations?"

"Not long. An Earth week, perhaps? That should be enough time to find what I need and travel back here in time to challenge Jaxson and the federation's board."

"My Queen, I am uncertain if a week of Earth's time will be enough."

"Doesn't their cycle work like ours?"

"No, it does not. Time is different there. It is hard for me to explain, but you will see a day pass with both light and dark. When it is dark, you will know that a day has passed, and little activity happens until the sun rises the next day. Their moon cycles take 30 days of light and dark."

"But it still sounds like it will take less than a cycle

to gain someone with a viable seed."

"I'm sure you are right, my Queen. I will prepare your ship, but are you sure you don't want me to travel with you?"

Tilda brushed some loose strands of Verena's chestnut locks from Verena's cheek.

"You've grown up so fast and so strong, Verena. I understand you may not need me as much as you once did, but you can't blame me for wanting to come and help."

"Tilda," Verena started as she took Tilda's hand, cupping her cheek, and placed it in hers. "You have been the mother I haven't had for many years, and I can't thank you enough for your devotion and love. But I need you here for our planet in my absence. Even though the Valet de Chambre made Jaxson swear to a truce for this whole heir business, I do not trust that he will keep to that promise. Until I am with child, I wouldn't put it past him to attack in my absence. And it would break my heart, as it would yours, to come home to that kind of loss. Please see that our people are safe and continue to train for the next battle."

"Yes, your Majesty. I will."

Tilda bowed her head slightly and smiled as she cupped Verena's face once more.

"And please make sure that you come back to us safely. The Earthlings may be primitive, but that doesn't mean they are tame by any stretch of the means."

"I understand, Tilda."

Laying Claim to the Lion

CHAPTER TWO

"You must strike while they aren't expecting it, my Liege. The treaty merely states—"

"The treaty merely states that we shall not attack while Verena is looking for a suitor, and I will not break the treaty while she does."

Jaxson beat his fist onto the desk in front of him. It was a light oak plain top with wrought iron legs fashioned in the shape of antlers.

"But Sire, her planet is the only other besides Tatsu that isn't under your reign. And without her and the help of the Effeminate warriors, we could never defeat the dragon shifters on our own. We must strike now while Effeminate is weak."

"Burchard, I will not hear any more of this. I want Verena as my queen, and I cannot have her if we overtake her planet."

"With all due respect, your Majesty, it may be best

to take her by force. She's a valiant opponent and should appreciate your strength as a mate."

"I don't want just her respect, Burchard,"

Jaxson's eyes narrowed, and he clenched his fists. Burchard's eyes widened.

"You've fallen in love with the woman, haven't you?"

"That is not your concern, Burchard! Now leave me be so I can look over the strategies you put before me!"

"But Sire, these are strategies for overthrowing planet Effeminate. You just said—"

"I know what I said, Burchard! Now leave me! I have much to think about. Peace treaty or not, we will still resume the war in 30 moon cycles!"

"As you wish, your Majesty."

Jaxson waited for Burchard to close the thick oak door behind him before he let out the breath he was holding in.

What am I going to do? I can't keep denying what I'm feeling. Everyone else knows it. It's not like I'm hiding my attraction to Verena all that well.

Jaxson brushed his fingers through his thick and dark locks and let out a sigh.

It's just that whenever I think of her, she makes me crazy. And if her parents betrothed her to me as they had promised, we wouldn't have had to wage this war. She would have already been mine.

Jaxson let out another breath and pinched the bridge of his nose with his thumb and forefinger.

Great! Another headache! It's all because I've been thinking of her and figuring out how to get her to love me back.

He went over to the window of his meeting room and looked out over the thickly forested area where his people like to hunt. He let out a sigh as he thought about his people trying to take out Verena's pride once more, as they had done during the Battle of Quell.

It was one of the few times his people had come together and fought as one. Before that battle, it proved hard for him to get his people to agree on any common ground. They were all loners and only saw fit to fight when it pleased them. They had never done a thing as a collective before. He even wondered if they would ever do anything as a collective again. Quell was five years ago. And though there were minor battles between Emir and Effeminate since then, those were all minor. Quell was the only major battle fought on Effeminate, and both sides lost a lot of warriors. Emir had fought well and almost won Effeminate, but the other planets in the solar system were easy to take. Their planets had been weak armies, outnumbered, and more self-centered than his people.

The thing was, if he ever had hopes of promising mates to his people, he had to overthrow Verena and planet Effeminate, and somehow this was bothering him. He didn't want to defeat her. He wanted her to reign by his side. Jaxson wished to claim her, take her as his own, to produce an heir that would unite their two kingdoms.

No woman should have to go through life without a mate, just as no man should have to, either. That was the natural order of things on Emir, so he found it challenging to understand Effeminate's all-female planet. Not one lion stayed with a mate on that planet except Verena's mother. Sadly, Verena didn't seem to share her mother's thoughts on companionship.

Still, something had to be done to unite the two planets because a panther-lion shifter would make a new and powerful race. A lion's pride and cunning prowess that could easily lead a battle would serve his elusive and adaptable panthers well, both on the battlefield and in the bedroom. Emir's resources became scarce around the capital. So he knew her lionesses would know precisely what his panthers would need to attain their prey further out in the jungle of their planet. The idea had his heart swelling.

It was still a perfect plan to claim her. And one that Jaxson had been set on since the day he laid eyes on Verena some 364 moon cycles ago when his parents and hers were in peace talks. She was nothing more than a cub like himself, but his territorial cunningness wanted her all to himself, and that was the day he vowed to take her as his own.

Jaxson looked out his window, which overlooked his entire kingdom. He smiled as his eyes gazed upon the thick trees of the land. He used to love climbing them when he was younger, just to think, and Jaxson remembered taking Verena up there when he was a cub. She hated climbing. Of course, no lion likes it.

But he enjoyed showing her his world. They shared their first kiss that day, and he hoped to share so much more with her.

He gazed over at the bookshelf that had a picture of the two of them climbing a tree together when they were kids. Jaxson walked over to it and took it down to get a closer look at the prize he intended to claim. As he traced over her picture, he searched to remember what it was like being so close to her body. They only kissed that one time, but it was something that still stuck with him, even after all these moon cycles.

Jaxson let out a sigh.

If only I could get her to see that we are perfect for one another.

He stroked the picture once more and smiled.

I'll talk to her again. Convince her the gods to believe them to be destined mates. And I should do it now, so she doesn't find a mate anywhere else like that stupid law wants her to do. I should be the one to give her an heir. Panthers and lions would be perfect as one!

"Burchard! Prepare my ship! I want to set a course for planet Effeminate tonight."

"Yes, Sire."

Acknowledgments

There are just too many of you now! So let me start with my bestie Karen.

Karen, you are sometimes "The Wind Beneath My Wings" because you've always been there to lift me up, even through the choppy waters in life. Your calmness in any given situation and your loyalty to listening have always helped me to float above water.

Sarah, my breath of fresh air, my floating line guiding me through everything new in my publishing world: PM—Post Mom. You've been my cheerleader, friend, and confidant in all this new mess I'm searching through in my second wave of life. You've taught me how to gain a sense of inner peace, and I cannot thank you enough for that!

Dale, I love you to death! You've been a beacon, a bestie, and a warrior in this writing business with me. You've reminded me of things I'd long forgotten and showed them to me with fresh eyes. You rock in so many ways for me, and for this, I thank you.

Christie, there are a whole lot of words I can say at this point in our 20-some-odd year climb in this biz! SHH! They don't need the exact year—we are still young in many people's eyes, after all! You've always,

always been a buoy in my life when I've needed you. Either you wind up reaching out to me—or I do you. We've led a very similar path. I'm so grateful for our chats in PMs and on video because it's helped me push through some of the more difficult writing blocks I've had over the years. You've helped me clear my mind so much so that I've got a better bearing on my work. I cannot thank you enough for the weekly talks!

Lastly, I'd like to thank my family that has passed. Mainly my mom, my uncle, which is her twin, and grandma and grandpa. You are all still that lighthouse I look to when navigating through the sometimes murky waters of this life. Thank you all for being there to shape me into the woman I've become.

9 798215 587423